The Knight's Kiss

SALLY NICHOLLS

With illustrations by
Nadiyah Suyatna

Barrington Stoke

To all th... ...me.

First published in 2022 in Great Britain by
Barrington Stoke Ltd
18 Walker Street, Edinburgh, EH3 7LP

www.barringtonstoke.co.uk

This edition based on *A Lily, A Rose*
(Barrington Stoke, 2013)

A CIP catalogue record for this book is available
from the British Library upon request

ISBN: 978-1-80090-163-6

Printed by Hussar Books, Poland

Contents

CHAPTER 1
FRIENDS

When I was fourteen, my cousin Dan was my favourite person in the whole world.

Dan came to my father's castle when I was thirteen. He was going to be a knight when he grew up, and his parents sent him to live with us to learn about fighting from Father.

Father was a knight. When I was little, he was away most of the time, fighting in the war against Robert the Bruce and the Scots. But when our new king, King Edward, was crowned, Father came back home.

I was happy to have him home. My mother died when I was small, so I was very lonely when Father was away at war.

I didn't know many people my own age. Before Dan came, my best friends were my maid, Alice, and my horse, Moonlight. I loved Alice and Moonlight, but horses can't talk, and Alice was very bossy. She wanted me to act like a lady.

That's because I am a lady. I am Lady Elinor of Hardford Castle, but I didn't feel like a lady then. Most of the time, I felt like a little girl.

Fourteen is too young to be a proper lady.

When Dan came, I was so happy. We did everything together. We went riding and hunting. We played dice and chess in the evenings. It was lovely to have a friend the same age as me.

One evening, we were all in the parlour. Dan and I were playing chess. I loved chess. I could play it all day long and be happy.

But Dan liked dice better. "I don't see why we always play chess," he grumbled. "You *always* win."

"That's because I'm better than you are," I told him. "I'm better than you at everything! I'm better at riding – and hunting – and dancing—"

"Elinor," said Alice. "Behave yourself. Ladies don't boast."

I stuck out my tongue. Dan giggled.

"I'll always be better than you," I told him. "You'll never beat me!"

"Want to bet?" he asked.

"Bet what?" I said. "That I'll always be better at everything?"

"No," said Dan. "That you'll win this game of chess."

Had he gone mad?

"Let's bet," said Dan. "If I win, you have to give me something. And if you win, I'll give something to you."

"Like what?" I asked. It sounded like a trick to me.

"Something nice," said Dan. "The loser can choose what they give. But it has to be something good."

"All right," I said.

That evening, Dan played *really* badly.

"Are you *trying* to lose?" I asked.

"No!" Dan said. But he lost anyway.

"I won!" I shouted. "I won! What do I get? What do I get?"

But Dan didn't tell me.

"Not here," he said. "It's a secret. I'll give it to you tomorrow, after lessons."

Every morning, I had lessons with Father Henry, who was the priest in our castle. I learned Latin and Greek and English and all about God and Jesus. Dan learned knight things, like shooting and fighting with a sword and jousting with my father.

After lessons, I went to the yard to help Dan put the bows and arrows away.

"Where's my present then?" I said. "Is it ready?"

"It's ready," said Dan. Suddenly, he looked nervous. "Close your eyes."

I closed my eyes and held out my hands. But Dan didn't put anything in them.

He kissed me, on the cheek.

CHAPTER 2
SECRETS

I was so shocked. I opened my eyes and just looked at him.

"What did you do that for?" I asked.

"Because ..." said Dan. He looked shy. "Because I love you."

"You *love* me?" I said.

"Yes. I do."

I was amazed. Dan loved me! How wonderful!

"Did you like it?" he said. "Being kissed?"

"Well ..." I felt myself go red. "Well, yes. I did like it."

"Good," said Dan. He kissed me again.

And that's how Dan and I fell in love.

I loved being in love with Dan. It was my secret, a secret only Dan and I – and Alice – knew.

I thought about Dan all the time. I'd be working, or eating, or helping Alice, and I'd think *I'm in love with Dan*, and it was as if my whole body would start smiling.

After dinner one evening, I went riding with Dan. I rode Moonlight fast up the road from the castle. Dan galloped behind me.

We rode through the forest and back home over Father's fields. It was cold, and the sky was a pale white-blue. The sun was setting behind us.

We led the horses back into the stables.

"Will you love me for ever?" Dan asked as he unbuckled his horse's saddle.

"I don't know," I said. I loved joking with him. "Will I love you when you're old and grey and boring?"

"I'll love *you* when you're old and grey and boring," said Dan. "I'll love *you* when you can't see any more and you've got no teeth."

"Yuck!" I said. "If your teeth fall out, I won't love you – I'll get someone better."

"You wouldn't really," said Dan. "Would you?" But I just laughed.

"*I'll* love you for ever," said Dan. "*I* can't imagine not loving you."

I thought for a moment.

"I can't imagine not loving you either," I said.

Dan smiled. He looked so sweet and happy that I leaned forwards and kissed him, on the mouth.

Dan blinked. But then he kissed me back.

We kissed. And kissed.

The door opened behind us.

It was Father.

CHAPTER 3
ANGRY

Father stood in the stable doorway, just looking at me and Dan. Then he marched over and grabbed my arm.

"What are you doing?" I said. "Let me go!"

"Come with me," said Father. "Right now."

I'd never seen him look so angry before.

Father dragged me out of the stable and across the yard. He pulled open the wooden door of the North Tower and pushed me up the stairs and into his room.

"How long has this been going on?" he growled. His voice was low and angry.

"It's nothing to do with you!" I said.

Father's face was purple.

"It has *everything* to do with me," he shouted. "I'm your *father*. Do you know what would happen to you if people found out you'd been kissing Dan in the stables? Who do you think would want to marry you then?"

"I don't care!" I said. "I wouldn't want to marry them either! I want to marry Dan!"

"Ha!" said Father. "Well, let's be clear on one thing, my girl. Dan's father will never let him marry you. Dan needs to marry a girl with money – you know that. And you need to marry a man who is friends with the King."

I was so angry I was nearly crying.

"I don't care what you want," I shouted. "We'll run away together and get married, and you can't stop us!"

"If you do," said Father, "you will have to become a nun. I will put you in a nunnery and never speak to you again."

We glared at each other.

"You are not to speak to Dan again," said Father. "You are not to go out riding with him. When you're not in lessons or at meals, you are to have Alice with you at all times. I'll tell her."

"But—" I said.

"Be quiet!" Father shouted. "Get out of my room."

I turned and ran out of the room crying.

*

The next two weeks were horrible.

Father was so angry. Dan and I weren't allowed to be alone together, ever.

Alice and I fought every day.

"I need to see Dan," I said.

"No, Elinor." Alice shook her head.

"But why *not*? You could watch us. We wouldn't do anything."

"Elinor, no." Alice was firm. "Your father would be so angry if he found out. He'd send me away. I'd lose my job."

"Aargh!" I kicked the bedpost and the whole bed shook. "Please, Alice. Please, please, please, please, *please*. I just want to talk to him. That's all."

"I'm sorry, Elinor." Alice did look sorry. "The answer's no."

"I hate you!" I shouted.

There was a knock at the door.

It was one of Father's servants.

"Lady Elinor," he said. "Your father wants to see you. He has some news for you."

CHAPTER 4
A PLAN

Father was in his room, writing. He looked up as I opened the door.

"Elinor," he said. "My darling. How are you?"

For the first time in weeks, he didn't sound angry.

"I'm still here," I said stiffly.

"Good," said Father. Then he took a deep breath.

"I have some news for you, Elinor," he said. "You're going to be married."

Married! Me, married!

"Who to?" I asked.

"His name is Sir William of Hale," said Father. "We fought together in Scotland. He's a good man."

I didn't say a word. I felt like I was going to cry.

"How old is he?" I asked at last.

"How old?" Father looked surprised. "About as old as I am."

"And – is he handsome?"

"Handsome!" Father laughed. "What do you think? He's a grown man, Elinor. He's got greying hair and a beard. He's a good man. That's what's important."

I didn't know what to say. I always knew Father would find me a husband one day. But not yet! Not so soon!

How could I marry an old man Father's age?

"I won't do it," I said.

"What did you say?"

"I won't do it," I said again. "I won't. I can't. I'm in love with Dan."

Father's face went pink.

"This is nonsense!" he said. "You and Dan are not going to *ever* be married."

I was angry too. "If you make me do this," I said, "I'll be so horrible to Sir William that he won't want to marry me."

Father's face went as red as a plum.

"Sir William is coming here on Monday to meet you," he said, his voice low. "If you so much as frown at him, I'll send Dan back to his father, and you'll never see him again. I mean it, Elinor."

"Please," I said. "Please, please, Father, don't make me get married. Not to an old man. I'm too young. I'm only fourteen. Let me stay here, just for a little bit longer. Please!"

Father sighed.

"I'm not trying to hurt you," he said. "I'm trying to look after you. This new king doesn't like our family very much, and we need all the friends we can get. Sir William will take care of you."

But I knew that if I couldn't be with Dan, I'd never be happy.

Never, never, never, never, never!

I'd just have to think of a plan.

I could do it.

I had to.

CHAPTER 5
A LOVER

On Monday, before supper, Alice combed my

hair and helped me into my best silk dress.

In the yard, I could hear horses and men's

voices. Sir William was here. I was frightened.

I felt trapped.

The great hall was dark. The fire was

burning in the middle of the room. Father and

Dan and Father Henry sat at the high table

with a man I didn't know. His skin was grey
and lined. He must have been nearly fifty. He

stood up as we came into the room, and so did Father.

"Sir William," Father said. "This is my daughter, Elinor. Elinor, this is Sir William."

"Delighted to meet you," said Sir William. He bowed.

"Delighted to meet you too," I said.

I sat down next to him.

"This must be very strange for you," said Sir William.

I nodded. "Yes, sir," I said.

"It's a little strange for me too," Sir William said. "I have a daughter your age. You're younger than my son."

I didn't answer.

"Come," said my nearly-husband. "Don't be shy. Tell me about yourself."

"I don't know what to tell you, sir," I said, looking down. *I wish you were dead* was all I could think of to say.

"Well," said Sir William. "What do you like to do? Do you like to ride?"

"Yes," I said. "And hunt."

"Good," said Sir William. "You'll be able to hunt when you live at my castle. And ride. What else? Do you play dice?"

"Yes, sir," I said. "And chess."

"Oh, chess." Sir William smiled. "My children like chess. We must play together sometime."

"Of course." I bowed my head.

"The castle where I live is right on the edge of England," said Sir William. "It's by the sea. You can ride along the beach and hunt in the forests. There are several other families nearby with girls your age. You'll make

friends. You must get very lonely living here,
so far away from anyone else."

"I don't mind," I said, but what he'd said
interested me. I'd never seen the sea before.
I'd never had friends my own age – apart from
Dan. Then I remembered that I was supposed
to hate Sir William, and I looked down.

When supper was over, Father and I walked up the stairs together.

"Well?" said Father quietly.

I didn't answer. I wanted to tell him that I hated Sir William, but I knew he wouldn't believe me.

I didn't hate him.

I didn't want to marry him.

But it looked like I had no choice.

CHAPTER 6
A KISS

We sat in the parlour all evening. I had to play the harp and sing. Everyone said I looked lovely, but after that they ignored me.

All the time, I was looking at Dan and thinking, *I wish I could talk to you.* He was looking at me too.

Then I thought of a way to see him.

It was dangerous, but I had to do it. I had to talk to Dan.

That night, I lay awake in bed and waited until I was sure Alice was asleep. Then I got up, carefully so as not to wake her.

I tiptoed out of our room and into the corridor. Night was my best chance of seeing

Dan. But he slept upstairs in a big room with other men – Father's servants. How was I going to get in there without waking one of them up?

It didn't matter. I had to try.

I walked – slowly, slowly, oh so slowly – up to his bedroom door. I pushed it open very gently.

Someone was awake in the room. I could see a person-shaped shadow coming towards me.

If I ran, the person would see me, but there was nowhere I could hide. I stepped

back into the corridor and closed the door as softly as I could.

The door opened. A voice said, "Hello?"

It was Dan.

"Dan!" I said. "It's me! Elinor!"

"Elinor!" His arms were around me, and we were kissing, and I felt like I was melting, like I was sinking into his skin.

"I love you," Dan whispered. "I love you so much."

"I love you too," I said. I said it over and over and over.

We kissed. And again. And again.

"You aren't going to marry him, are you?" Dan said.

"I don't know," I said. "I can't see what else I can do."

"I *hate* him," said Dan. His voice was low and angry. "I'll *kill* him if he takes you away."

"No, you won't," I said. What a stupid idea!

Dan wouldn't really do it. He was just playing at being an outlaw.

But it was too late for playing.

This was for real.

*

Sir William stayed with us for three days.

On the second day, Alice and I were coming upstairs after a ride when I saw Sir William writing a letter in the parlour. He smiled at me.

"Come and sit with me," he said. He nodded at Alice, who went upstairs.

I came into the parlour and sat on the chair beside him.

"Don't look so shy," he said. He was kind. "A husband and wife should be friends. I thought maybe you could read to me. Or play chess, perhaps?"

And that's when I had my idea.

"Let's play chess," I said. "And if I win, you give me a present."

Sir William looked surprised. Until now, I'd been so quiet. He didn't expect me to start asking for things.

"And what if you lose?" he said.

"If I lose," I said, "I'll give you a kiss."

CHAPTER 7
A CHESS PLAYER

I loved chess. It was my favourite thing. Better than riding. Better than hunting.

For the first time in weeks, I didn't feel stupid, or shy, or scared. I felt like myself.

I stopped worrying about Sir William, and I stopped worrying about Dan. I just thought about the game.

Sir William was good at chess. But he wasn't as good as I was.

"Check," I said.

That meant his king was in danger. If he moved it to the right, he'd escape. If he moved it left, I could beat him.

Sir William picked up his king. He moved it left.

Yes!

"Checkmate," I said.

I'd won!

Sir William was smiling, but he looked surprised.

"So, what would you like?" Sir William asked. "A new horse? All my gold?"

I bit my lip. Sir William was a good man. Everyone said so.

"Please," I said. "Please, sir, don't ask me to marry you. I'm too young to look after a home. I don't want to leave my father, not yet."

"I see." Sir William was quiet for a moment. Then he said, "Elinor, you do understand how important it is for our families to be joined, don't you?"

"I know," I said. "But not yet, please. I know I'm asking a lot, sir, but please."

Sir William sighed. "Let me think about it," he said. "But I can't make you any promises."

"I know," I said. My face was hot. I felt stupid – like a child. "Thank you, sir."

*

After supper, Father called me. "Elinor, can I talk to you, please?"

We went into his writing room. *This is it*, I thought. *My last chance.*

Father said, "I talked to Sir William this afternoon."

"Yes?"

"He thinks you're a clever young woman," said Father. "He liked you a lot. But he thinks you're too young to run a home."

My heart started to thump.

"He needs an older wife," said Father.

"So I don't have to be married?" I asked.

"Slow down." Father smiled at me. "Sir William and I both very much want our families to be joined. Sir William would like you to be married to his son, Adam," said Father.

His son!

"Adam is sixteen," Father said. "He's a squire, like Dan. Soon he'll be a knight." Father smiled, but I couldn't smile back. I was too shocked.

This was a good thing Sir William had given me. He was a kind man. I ought to be happy. But all I could think of was Dan.

"Sir William says," Father added, smiling a little, "that he thinks you'll like Adam. He's an excellent chess player."

CHAPTER 8
A PRIZE

Sir William left the next day. He was going to see his son and then bring him back here so we could meet each other.

One month ago I was going to marry Dan.

One week ago I was going to marry Sir William.

Now I was going to marry Adam.

It was all too quick. I didn't know how to feel.

*

I was reading with Father Henry when Sir William and his son arrived a few days later. Alice knocked on the door.

"They're here," she said. "Your father wants you to come and meet them."

Father was in the parlour with Sir William. He looked up and smiled as we came in.

"And here's Elinor! Doesn't she look lovely?" said Father.

"Very lovely," said Sir William. "Elinor, this is my son, Adam."

I bobbed down, keeping my eyes low. Then I looked up.

Adam was tall, taller than Dan. He was long and lanky, with big feet and big hands and a big mouth. He was smiling. He wasn't as handsome as Dan ... but he looked kind.

"I'm very pleased to meet you," he said, and he bowed.

I looked at him again. He was carrying a falcon on his wrist.

"What a beautiful bird!" I said.

He smiled at me. "Her name is Joanne. She's a merlin."

"I know," I said. "My bird is a merlin too."

"You hunt?" He looked surprised, and so pleased that I nearly laughed. "Is there good hunting here?"

"Very. Perhaps you can hunt with us this afternoon."

"I'd like that very much," said Adam.

I looked down at my hands. We were both quiet. I kept looking sideways at him out of the corner of my eye.

The second time I did it, he caught my eye and laughed. I blushed.

"I'm sorry," he said. "I didn't mean to make you nervous. Isn't this an odd way to meet each other? My father only told me about you yesterday."

"Did he tell you why he wants us to be married?" I asked.

"Yes." Adam smiled. "He was very impressed with you. I hope you like me. What will you do to me if you don't?"

I smiled back at him.

"I haven't decided yet," I said.

We smiled at each other. My heart started beating faster. *He likes me*, I thought. *I know he does. And – what's more – I think I like him too.*

*

That afternoon, we went hunting. Father, Sir William, Adam and I.

Adam was a better rider than Dan. He didn't know the forest so well, but he could ride as fast as I could. He was a good falconer too. He let his falcon fly at the right time and it caught a hare.

When we went in to supper, Adam talked to Father about his horse, his falcon, his plans. I could see that Father liked him.

I sat and listened. What should I do? I loved Dan, and yet I understood why Father would never let us marry.

So perhaps I should stop wishing for the impossible. Perhaps I should take the man I'd been given and be thankful.

CHAPTER 9
DANCING

Things were changing.

Dan was going back home to live with his father. Soon he would be made a knight.

"My father's going to Scotland, to fight for King Edward," he told me.

"Will you go too?" I asked.

He shrugged. "Maybe. What do you care?"

Dan was angry with me. Angry because I was going to marry Adam. Angry because I didn't fight harder to marry him. Angry because he thought I didn't love him any more.

I did love him. I did.

I just …

I thought I might love Adam as well.

Just a little bit.

*

Three months later, Adam and I were married in our castle chapel. Father Henry said the words.

Afterwards, we had a feast. There was music and dancing. I stood and watched the dancers. Dan was standing by the door, looking out. My heart jumped. I was sad to see him so unhappy.

I went and stood beside him. I wanted to touch him, but I didn't.

"Let's be friends at least," I said, but he turned away and gave a shrug.

"Friends," he said bitterly. "A few months ago, you said you loved me more than anyone else in the world. Now you just want to be friends!"

"I still love you," I said. "Dan! I do!"

"If you say so," he said, and he turned away.

Inside the hall, the musicians were still playing. Adam came and stood beside me. He had a big smile on his face.

"Happy?" he said.

"Yes," I said. Was I telling the truth? I wasn't sure.

"What were you talking to Dan about?" he asked.

"Nothing, really," I said.

Adam frowned. He didn't believe me.

"He's angry with me," I said. "He ... we ... we used to love each other. He didn't want me to marry you."

Adam looked worried.

"Do you still love him?" he said.

"I don't know," I said. "No, I do know. I do love him. But ... I'm married now. Dan and

I – that's over. I want to be a good wife, and I think you and I could be happy together. And we can't be happy if I'm still wanting Dan, can we?"

"No," said Adam. He looked thoughtful. "I was in love once," he said.

"Oh yes?" I was surprised by how jealous I felt.

"Her name was Christine." He laughed. "Her father was a farmer in our village. I used to watch her in church every Sunday. I never spoke to her."

I laughed too.

"We'll be all right together," I said.
"Won't we?"

"We will," he said. "I promise."

"I promise too." I took his hand. "Shall
we dance?"

Our books are tested
for children and young people by
children and young people.

Thanks to everyone who consulted on
a manuscript for their time and effort in
helping us to make our books better
for our readers.